MW00981956

Annie Ashcraft Looks Into the Dark

Ruth Senter

ILLUSTRATED BY

Lee Christiansen

Annie Ashcraft Looks Into the Dark

Design and Production: Lookout Design Group (www.lookoutdesign.com)

Printed in China.

Library of Congress Cataloging-in-Publication Data

CIP Data applied for.

"I can lie down and go to sleep. And I will wake up again because the Lord protects me."

Psalm 3:5

INTERNATIONAL CHILDREN'S BIBLE

To Nicky, who has waited a very long time for this book.

–R.S.

For my mom and dad.

–L.C.

Annie is small, and the night is big. Very big. And sometimes scary. Tonight the night looks like it's watching her, like white eyes peeking through the dark. And there are noises—like the kind coming at her now from the other side of the thin, knotty-pine walls of her bedroom. *Scrape. Scritch. Scrape.* As though something with claws is trying to get in.

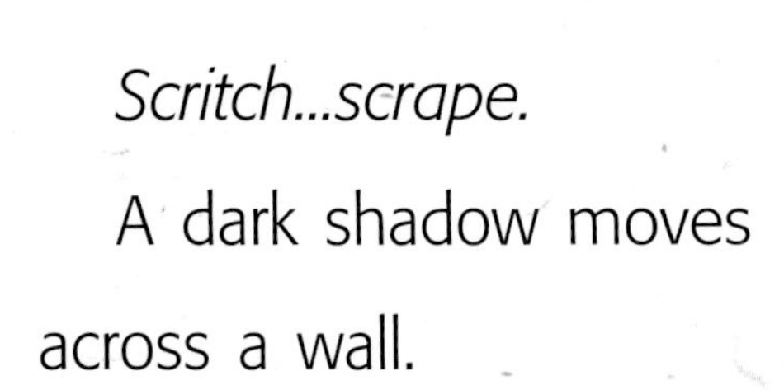

Scritch...scrape.

A dark shadow moves across a wall.

THE LORD IS MY
SHEPHERD

Annie pulls her blue-and-white quilt over her head and buries herself into its warmth. But the quilt cannot keep out the scraping noise on the other side of the wall.

Scritch...SCRAPE.

Annie is too scared to move. She shivers even though it is summer. She's glad her mother closed the window before she went to bed. Now at least whatever is outside making that awful noise can't get in.

But the latched window doesn't keep out the scary noise. Neither does the quilt. Nor Annie's pillow. Nor her eyes, which are squinted shut so tightly they hurt.

Scritch...SCRAPE.

SCRITCH...SCRAPE.

Is the noise coming closer? Will it come through the pine walls and closed window?

Annie sits straight up in bed, goose pimples rising on her arms like so many knots on a tree.

"D-a-d-d-y!" She barely squeaks out the word.

"D-a-d-d-y!" She doesn't dare say it too loudly. Whatever it is on the other side of the wall will surely know she's scared.

"D-a-d-d-y!"

Somehow Daddy hears. And he is there, bundling her up, quilt and all, holding her close.

She snuggles into his warm, safe arms.

But still Annie worries about the thing outside her window. She doesn't like it that Brownie, her cocker spaniel, is locked up in the barn, down a small lane that goes from the back of the house, past the outhouse, through the gate, and alongside the chicken coop. Brownie is out there all by himself.

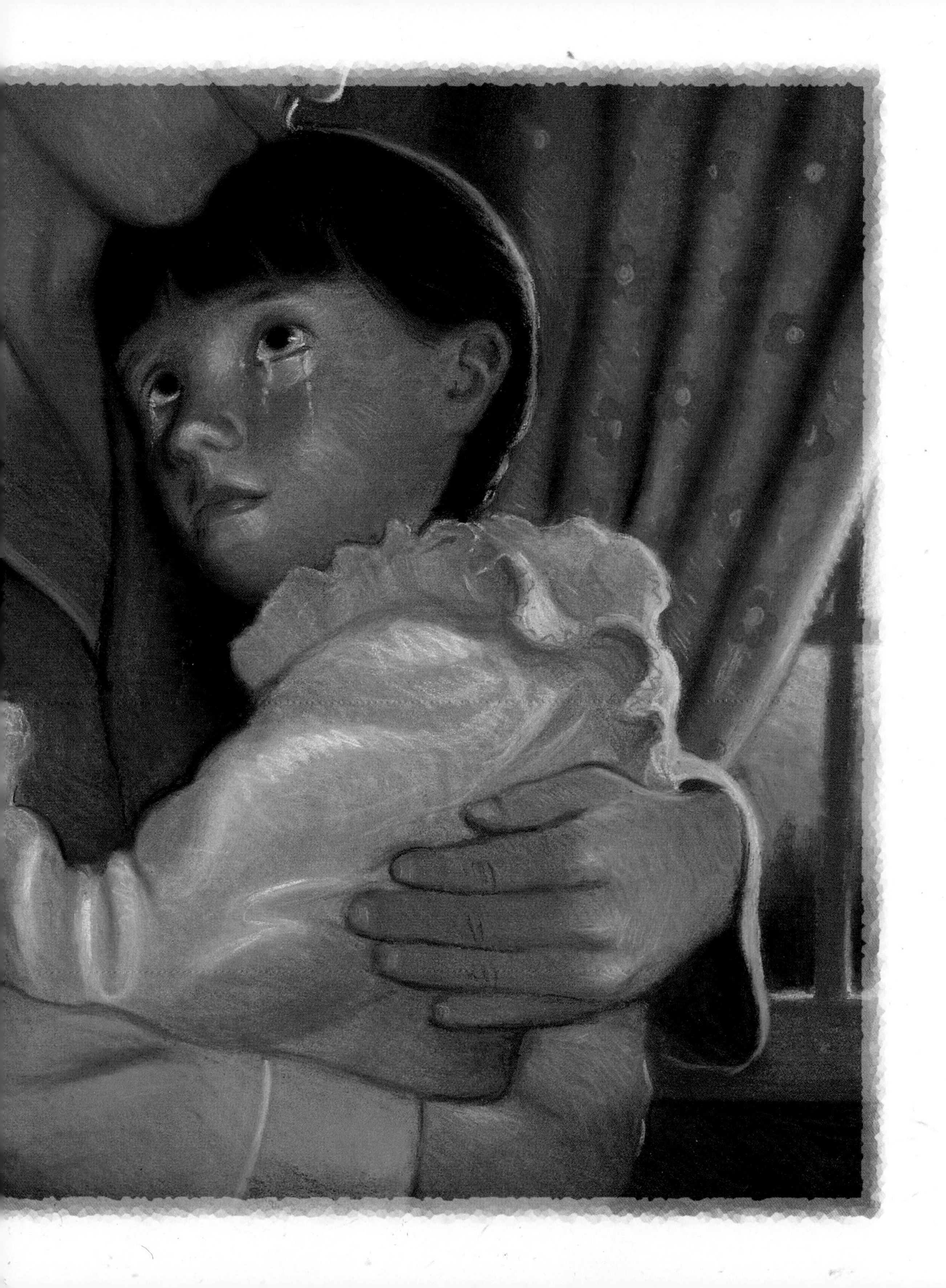

Hot tears start to run down Annie's cheeks in a steady stream.

"D-a-d-d-y, the trees are moaning. The night is scraping. It's soooo scary out there."

Daddy holds her close and lets her cry. Then he brushes the hair out of her eyes and wipes her wet cheeks with his fingers.

"Let's go look out the window and see what's there," he suggests softly.

Annie's eyes grow wide. She does not want to look out the window. That is where the *scritching, scraping* noises are coming from. She would rather Daddy carry her into her parents' bedroom and tuck her into bed between himself and her mother as he has done so often before when she is frightened.

"Daddy, please...I don't want to look. Can't I just sleep with you and Mommy? Can't we just move someplace less scary, like back east to Grandma and Grandpa, where the houses are closer together and there are no woods?"

Her daddy gently carries her to the window and pulls back the curtains. His voice is quiet and firm.

"Honey, you are growing up now. You can't always run to our bed, and we can't move back east. Even though it doesn't always seem like it, God is with us wherever we are."

He takes a deep breath, and she can feel his heart beating next to hers.

"Now, let's see if we can find where that noise is coming from."

Daddy peers into the dark.

"Oh, Annie," he says, "look at this moonlight! See all the things you love. Your swing. The apple tree you like to climb. Our little log cabin where I study and you take naps in front of the fire. And the barn. Remember how much fun you had today sliding down the hay?"

Annie leans forward, just a little. "But...what is that noise?" she whispers.

Daddy listens hard now, his ear almost touching the window.

Annie watches his eyes move across the darkness. Suddenly, they stop.

"Well, what do you know.... Look at that little door on the gas pump, Annie. It's trying to come open, rubbing against the chain I use to lock up the pump at night."

Annie can see the white teeth of his smile.

"There is your noise."

And then, with her daddy, Annie looks into the dark. She sees the noisy gas pump, silhouetted against the night. She sees the swing and the apple tree and the log cabin and the barn and fluffy clouds scuttling across the sky.

Annie sighs, long and deep.

"And now, young lady,
I think it's time you climb
back into bed. Or morning
will be here before you've
even closed your eyes."

Daddy carries her back to
bed, pulls the quilt up
around her chin, and kisses
her good-night for the
second time.

"I'll be right down the hall
if you need me again,"
he says as he moves like a
shadow through the doorway.

"Good night, Daddy,"
Annie says from under the
covers.

Scritch...scrape. The noise goes on.

But Annie snuggles peacefully at last, deep into her blue-and-white quilt and her soft bed, which is small but very, very safe.

And finally, she sleeps.